**King Triton**
*Ariel's father*

**Ursula**
*A wicked sea witch*

**Scuttle**
*A seagull*

**Max**
*Eric's dog*

**Flotsam and Jetsam**
*Servants to Ursula (two eels)*

*Trouble is in store for Ariel, mermaid daughter of Triton, ruler of the seas. She has fallen in love with a human prince! But her friends come to her help — even against the wicked sea witch...*

Designed by Michael Usher, using stills from the film.

British Library Cataloguing in Publication Data
Walt Disney's The little mermaid.
    I. Walt Disney Productions
    823'.914[J]
    ISBN 0-7214-1356-0

First edition

Printed in England

# WALT DISNEY'S
# THE LITTLE MERMAID

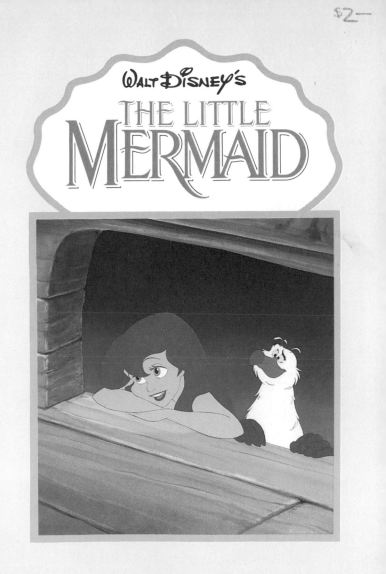

Ladybird Books

Once upon a time, there was a mermaid princess called Ariel. She was interested in humans. In those days, humans lived on land, and

merpeople lived in the sea. Merpeople had tails instead of legs, to help them to swim.

Ariel was always looking for things that had belonged to humans. One day, instead of singing at a concert given by her father, King Triton, she was hunting through a wrecked ship.

Triton was very cross. "Ariel needs watching," he told his servant Sebastian. "And you are just the crab to do it!"

A fish called Flounder went everywhere with Ariel. One day, the shadow of a ship loomed over them, and they both went up to look at it.

On board was Eric, a handsome prince, who was having a birthday party with the crew and his dog Max. Just as the crew gave Eric a statue of himself, the sky grew stormy and the wind rose. The ship was wrecked.

Everyone else was safe, but Eric nearly lost his life rescuing his dog from the doomed ship.

Ariel rushed to
help the young
prince, and took
him ashore. As she
sang to him in her
beautiful voice, he
slowly came back
to life, and she fell in love with him.

When Triton found out that Ariel
was in love with a human he was
angry. So angry that he destroyed
her collection of human things —
even the statue of Eric that
Flounder had saved from the wreck.

"Humans are savages," he told
his daughter. "They even eat fish!"

Triton had one great enemy –
Ursula, a sea witch. She wanted to
take over his kingdom of the sea.
When she heard about the family
quarrel, she saw her chance.

She would offer to help Ariel to
become human and marry her prince!

Sebastian was now friends with
Ariel. He and Flounder warned her
not to meet the evil Ursula,
but she wouldn't listen.
So they followed her, but
Flotsam and Jetsam, the eels
who worked for
Ursula, soon
stopped them.

The wicked sea witch made a bargain with Ariel. In exchange for Ariel's voice, the witch would give her legs — but only for three days.

"Do you understand?" asked Ursula.

"Eric must fall in love with you, and kiss you, before sunset on the third day."

Ariel was too happy to worry. Ursula told her again, "If you fail, your tail will come back and you will be in my power for ever."

But Ariel just smiled. She wasn't going to fail!

When Ariel set out to find her prince, Sebastian went with her. Another friend went too – it was Scuttle the seagull, who thought he knew all about humans. (Although he didn't – he said that humans used a *fork* to comb their hair!)

The moment Eric saw her, he knew Ariel was the maiden who had saved his life, even though she couldn't speak. He took her home to his palace, where the servants dressed her in fine clothes. Then he gave a great feast in her honour.

The second day of the magic spell dawned. Eric took Ariel for a drive in a golden carriage to show her his kingdom. Sebastian went along in her pocket, and Scuttle flew along overhead. They both tried all day to get Eric to kiss Ariel, but with no luck.

Later, as she danced the night away in Eric's arms, Ariel longed to tell him how happy she was. Sadly, she couldn't say a word — and he still didn't try to kiss her.

But Ursula the sea witch was afraid Ariel would succeed. She turned herself into a beautiful maiden – with Ariel's voice.

Her song drew Eric to her, and he fell under her wicked spell. He forgot all about Ariel. He told his servants, "Now I've found my true love, I'm going to marry her as quickly as possible, before I lose her again..."

Nearby, Sebastian and Scuttle listened, horrified. How could they stop this happening?

Scuttle brought all his friends from the seashore to help. There were birds, sea-lions, pelicans and even lobsters. There were so many of them and they made so much noise that the wedding couldn't go on.

Max bit the bride, and suddenly the spell was broken. Ursula began to croak.

Ariel got her voice back, and Eric at last knew *she* was his true love.

Too late, alas. The sun was setting. Ariel's legs turned into a tail and the sea witch dragged her beneath the waves.

Ursula cackled with glee. Now that she had Ariel, Triton would give her anything she wanted.

She was right. "You can have my crown, my kingdom and my trident," he cried. "Only give me back my beloved daughter."

The sea witch took the trident eagerly – then turned Triton into a small slimy creature, wriggling on the sea bed.

Next, she was
going to destroy
the merpeople!

Ariel was in despair. This was all her fault! But her friends helped her yet again.

They all turned on the sea witch and attacked her. Someone else helped as well – Eric. He had come to look for Ariel in his new ship.

Ursula hurriedly stirred up a whirlpool, but it was no use. She and her eels were crushed under the bows of Eric's ship. They would never cause trouble any more.

The trident Ursula had been carrying sank to the sea bed. Triton touched it and became king again.

Triton's kingdom beneath the waves was peaceful once more.

Only the mermaid princess Ariel was unhappy. She sat day after day on a rock dreaming of Eric.

At last her father said, "If you love him so much, I suppose you must marry him." So saying, he turned Ariel into a human and gave her a splendid wedding.

As Eric and his princess sailed away to live happily ever after, a rainbow suddenly appeared over the ship. It was one last gift from Triton, king of the sea.

**Ariel**
*The little mermaid*

**Eric**
*A human prince*

**Flounder**
*A fish*

**Sebastian**
*Servant to King Triton (a crab)*